BY CLAUDIA RECINOS SELDEEN

An imprint of Enslow Publishing
WEST 44 BOOKS™

Please visit our website, www.west44books.com.
For a free color catalog of all our high-quality books,
call toll free 1-800-398-2504.

Cataloging-in-Publication Data
Names: Seldeen, Claudia Recinos.
Title: Like and subscribe / Claudia Recinos Seldeen.
Description: Buffalo, NY : West 44, 2025. | Series: West 44 YA verse
Identifiers: ISBN 9781978597600 (pbk.) | ISBN 9781978597594 (library bound) | ISBN 9781978597617 (ebook)
Subjects: LCSH: Social media--Fiction. | Interpersonal relations--Fiction. | High school--Fiction. | Sisters--Fiction. | Infatuation--Fiction.
Classification: LCC PZ7.1.S453 Li 2025 | DDC [F]--dc23

First Edition

Published in 2025 by
Enslow Publishing LLC
2544 Clinton Street
Buffalo, New York 14224

Copyright © 2025 Enslow Publishing LLC

Editor: Caitie McAneney
Designer: Leslie Taylor

Photo Credits: Cover (holding hands) jacoblund/iStockphoto.com, (open book) Jure Divich/Shutterstock.com (like button) TMvectorart/Shutterstock, (subscribe button) Vlad Ra27/Shutterstock.com; Dedication page (emoji) KVASVECTOR/Shutterstock.com; (interior series art books) donatas1205/shutterstock.com.

All rights reserved. No part of this book may be reproduced in any form without permission in writing from the publisher, except by a reviewer.

Printed in the United States of America

CPSIA compliance information: Batch #CW25W44: For further information contact Enslow Publishing LLC at 1-800-398-2504.

For B.
Heart-eyes and heart emojis forever.

Seen

There are books
all over
my room.
        Scattered on my desk.
              Sliding off my nightstand.

Books fill the shelves
on my wall.
They're lined up like
souvenirs
from all the
imaginary places
I've been.

But in the corner
of my room,
there's a stack
of books
I never touch.
        Books with
        boring covers.
        Plain titles.

Sometimes
I lie in bed
and stare at those
unread books.
And I think how horrible
it must be.

To be ignored.
To be set aside.

It keeps me
up
at night.
The thought
that I might end up
like the books
in that pile.

Instead of
the popular books
that fly
off the shelves.

The ones that get
talked about.

The ones
that are
seen.

First Light

It's still dark
when I wake up
for school.

The first light I see
isn't the sun
streaming in
through my window.

The first light I see
is the glow
of my phone screen.

The first sound I hear
is the alarm app.
The opening bars
of my favorite song.

One

I rub the sleep
from my eyes.
Then I go through
my morning routine
on my phone.
         Email.
         Discord.
         Social media.

I take a deep breath
and check my video channel.
         My book review vlog.
         My pride and joy.

But a minute later I deflate
like an old balloon.

I posted a new video
last night.

But my video isn't
the breakout hit
I'd hoped for.

I don't have
any new subscribers.

The view count is a grand total
of one.

Traditions

I would love
to skip breakfast.

But our family
has traditions.

We always
open presents
on *Noche Buena*.
Christmas Eve.
      Right when the clock
      strikes midnight.

We always
say *good night*
before we go to bed.
      Even if we're angry.
      Even if we're tired.

And we always
have breakfast
together.

Rich and Famous

My little sister
perks up
as soon as I
sit down.

*Gabby has
a new video,*
she announces.

I narrow
my eyes
at her.

In return,
Elena grins.
        Button nose crinkled.
        Brown eyes squinted.
        Braces winking
        in the morning light.

Another video?
my dad asks.
He smooths his tie
and flashes
a smile.
*I hope you'll still talk to us
when you're
rich and famous.*

Elena rolls
her eyes.

My dad thinks
being on the internet
makes you famous.

But having
your own channel
isn't enough.

It's views
that matter.
It's followers
and engagement.
It's getting people
to watch your videos.

And then
getting them to
subscribe.

This Year

Elena is taking forever
to get in the car.

This wasn't a problem
last year.
When she was still in
middle school.
When I got a ride
with Mom,
and Elena
rode the school bus.

But this year,
I'm a sophomore.
Elena is a freshman.

This year
Elena is
everywhere.

Sister

I climb out
of the car.

*Don't forget
to help your sister,*
Mom calls.

I blow my bangs
out of my eyes
in frustration.
But I stop
and wait for Elena.

*Your backpack
is ridiculous,*
I inform her.

She does a little
hop.
Heaving the
boulder-sized bag
higher
on her shoulders.

I know,
she sighs.
*I've got a lot
of books in here.*

Main Office

We stop
at the main office
so Elena can pay
her band fees.

While we wait,
I lean
on the counter.
I play with the end
of my ponytail.
I let my attention
wander to the back.

    There's a table
    where the student aides
    hang out.

    Where Marco sits.
    Frowning down
    at his phone
    like he's a bronze statue.

    Like he's a work of art.

Marco Acosta

Marco Acosta
is a junior.

He has dark hair
that reminds me of
the ocean.
The way it
swoops and swirls.

His eyes
make me think
of hot chocolate
on snowy mornings.

His cheeks are—

What are you looking at?
Elena whispers.

I swallow a yelp.
Nothing, I mutter.

I dart a glance at Marco
to make sure
he didn't hear.

But Marco
isn't looking
at me.

Pretend

Before the bell rings,
the classroom
is a swarm
of sound.

I pull out
my notebook
and pretend
to write.
But I pay
close attention
to the chatter of voices.

*The homecoming game . . .
. . . a movie this weekend . . .
Marco's new vlog post . . .*

I pretend
I'm a scientist
taking it all in.

I pretend
I'm a spy.

I pretend
it doesn't matter
that no one talks
to me.

Lunch

Elena eats lunch
in the second floor
hallway.
Between the stairwell
and the music room.

I saw her once.
Sitting in a circle
with her band friends.

I eat lunch
in the library.
Between the new releases
and the mystery novels.

I eat lunch
by myself.

Record

After school,
I lock myself
in my room.

I open my laptop.
I open the video app.
I sweep my bangs
out of my eyes.

And I hit
"record."

My Channel

It seems like
almost everyone
at school
has their own
video channel.

I started mine
two months ago.

After summer
ended.

After school
began.

After Marco Acosta
started his gossip channel.
And it became
the most popular channel
in school.

The Problem

I hold up
the book I'm reviewing.
      A story about a boy
      who falls in love
      with a ghost.

The book is a bestseller.
It should generate views.
It should be easy.

The problem
is that I didn't like
the book.

The problem
is that I have
nothing to say.

The problem,
I sigh,
is that even a ghost
is better than I am
at getting people
to like her.

My Goal

I manage to put together
five minutes
of video.

It's not
my best work.
       It's not even
       good work.

But I have to post
regularly
to get followers.
       (I have
       two subscribers.
       And one of them
       is my mom.)

My goal is to be
internet famous.
       (Or at least
       internet well-known.)

So I upload my video.
Then I flip my laptop
closed.

Temporary

That night I lie in bed.
I try to come up with ways
to grow my channel.

But all
I can think about
is the mismatched-sock feeling
of walking into homeroom
every morning.
And not having
someone
to talk to.

I close my eyes
and tell myself
it's temporary.

Everything
will be different
when my channel
takes off.

When people
know
who I am.

Notification

My phone
whirs
from my nightstand.
And I
fumble
awake.

I sit up.
My eyelids heavy
with sleep.
But when I look at
my phone,
my drowsiness
vanishes.

I blink down
at the screen.

A notification
blinks back.

You have one new subscriber.

A Comment

My new subscriber
has a username:
Ghostboy.

My first thought
is that it must be
one of Elena's friends.
But they all have
silly,
band-related names.
        Like *Treblemaker*
        or *BabygotBach.*

My second thought
is that it must be
a spam account.
        Like my other
        subscriber.
        The one that's not
        my mom.

But then
I realize
my new subscriber
didn't just
follow.
They also
left a comment
on my latest video.

The one about
the ghost book.

Do you think it's easier,
to like a ghost?
the comment reads.
Than it is to like
a real live person?

That Means You

Elena perks up
the minute I walk
into the dining room.

*Gabby has
a new subscriber!*
she announces.

I freeze
halfway to the table.

What the heck, Elena?
I gasp.

She grins.
Wide enough
that I see
the pink rubber bands
on her braces.

Dad stands up.
He smiles
his toothpaste-ad smile.
*You girls
and your channels,*
he says.

He takes his suit jacket
carefully
off the back
of his chair
and slides it on.

Mom taps
one manicured nail
on the table.
Eat up girls,
she says.
*We don't want
to be late.*

I point at Elena.
That means you.

She makes a face.
Then she holds
my gaze
as she takes the
slowest
        bite
                ever.

What to Say

Elena sings
with the radio
all the way to school.

After a while
I get tired
of trying to tune her out.
I pull out my phone.
And check
my vlog.

I let out
a quiet sigh
of relief.

Nothing
has changed.
My new follower
is still there.

And so is their comment.

Internet Safety

I know all the rules
of internet safety.

I never share
personal information
in my videos.
>No passwords.
>No address or phone number.

I don't accept
chat requests
from people
I don't know.

I would never agree
to meet up with
anyone
I met online.

I know I don't
owe
Ghostboy
a response.
I tell myself
I'm not
even sure
I *want*
to respond.

But the truth is
I do.

I want to
answer
his question.

I want to
respond.

I'm just afraid
I'll say
the wrong thing.

Boat

Sitting in homeroom
is like sitting in
a boat.

I'm surrounded by
a sea of people.
Their voices
bounce
against me
like ocean waves.

I'm sitting
right in the middle
of it.

But I'm not
a part of it.

Even though
the faces around me
are familiar.
Even though
we've been going
to school together
for years.

Everybody is
bunched up
into tight little groups.
And there's
no space
for me.

So I sit in my boat.
I listen to
the sea of voices.
And I wonder
what it would be like
to dive in.

Dani and Gabby

It wasn't always
like this.

I used to have
someone to talk to.
Daniela.
("Dani")

Her mom was
best friends
with my mom.
So Dani and I
grew up like sisters.

We had the same dark hair.
The same thick bangs.
The same taste in clothes.

We were like
two halves
of a story.
Like two library books
sitting next to each other
on a shelf.

Dani and Gabby.
Gabby and Dani.

But last year,
Dani's dad
got a job in London.

Dani
moved away.

And I was left
behind.

I was left
alone.

Hush

The hush
of the library
is like the world
outside my window
after the first fall of snow.
        Muted.
        Muffled.
        Still.

I sit
in my usual lunch spot,
surrounded
by a wall
of books.
I dig my phone
out of my backpack.

Ghostboy's comment
waits for me
under my latest video.
    Do you think it's easier
    to like a ghost?

I type out
a reply.

Then I
delete it.

I take a bite
of my sandwich.

Ghostboy's comment
seems thoughtful.
Smart.

I want to make sure
I sound smart, too.

I put my sandwich down
with a sigh.
I start to tuck my phone
back in my
backpack.

But just then
it
pings
an alert.

> Marco Acosta
> has uploaded
> a new video.

Everyone

I subscribe
to Marco's channel.
>Everyone does.
>We all want to hear
>about the latest
>blowups,
>hookups,
>and breakups.

I watch Marco's videos
the moment
he uploads them.
>Everyone watches.
>For days,
>it's all anyone
>talks about.

Marco's rich voice
delivers the latest
school news.
He talks over pictures of
a stormy sky.
>A field of dandelions.
>>An empty playground.

He never appears
on camera
himself.

But that doesn't
stop me
from watching.

I want to know
what's happening.
Everyone does.

But
the truth is,
I would watch
Marco's channel.
Even if all he did
was talk about
paint drying.
   Dust settling.
      The stock market.

I would be glued
to my phone,
watching the pictures
play
across my screen.

Even if Marco
was as silent
as the world
after a snowstorm.

Marco's Words

I almost miss it.

I'm so distracted
by the background photograph of
a rainy parking lot.
Marco's words
almost
slip
right by me.

I sit up with a jerk.
I back the video up.

I'm wrong,
I tell myself.
I have to be
wrong . . .

But then I
hear it
again.

Elena's name.
On Marco's channel.

My Little Sister

Marco just told
the world
Elena is going
to homecoming.

Elena.
With the squinty eyes.
With the horrible
singing voice.

She's going with
Justin.
Marco's best
friend.

I frown.
I picture Elena
at the breakfast table.
Running to the car.
Fighting with
her backpack.

How did
my clumsy little sister
manage to get a date
with Justin?
And why is this
the first time
I'm hearing about it?

Ask Elena

I climb
into the car.
I slam the door
behind me.

How was school?
Mom asks.

I shrug.
Ask Elena.

My mom arches
an eyebrow.
She glances
in the rearview mirror
at Elena's reflection.
What's up?
she asks.

I fold my arms
across my chest.
I look out the window.

But I can still see
Elena's smile
in my head.
      The way her nose
      scrunches up.
      The flash of braces.

I can feel her smile
in the way
she grips
the back of my seat.

I can hear her smile
in her voice.
In the breathless way
she says Justin's name.
Over and over.

Someone I Don't Know

When we were kids,
Elena would
run
to my room
if she was scared
      of the dark
      or a thunderstorm
      or a nightmare.

I would sigh.
And let her
climb
under the covers.
      Even though
      she hogged the bed
      and kicked me
      in her sleep.

Because I'm
the big sister.
I'm the one who knows
how the world works.

But tonight
I walk into my room.
And I realize
it's been years
since Elena knocked
on my door.

I think about
her group of
friends.
The way they looked
that time I saw them
eating lunch.
The closed loop
they made.

I think about Elena
telling Mom
all about homecoming.
I didn't even know
she was going.
Much less with
Marco's best friend!

I think about
the way Elena's name
sounded
when Marco said it.

Like a word
I didn't
recognize.

Like someone
I don't
know.

Other Girls

I sit down
in front of my laptop
with the latest book
I want to
review.

But instead of
recording
a new vlog post,
I check
my social media.
I start
scrolling.
Past pictures of
takeout sandwiches.
Sleeping cats.
A concert stage.

I keep scrolling
until I come across
a picture of
a smiling girl.
And then
I freeze.

Dani's face
peers out at me
from my screen.

And my heart
snaps
like a rubber band.

Her bangs
have grown out.
She's wearing
lipstick.
But she still has
the same brown eyes.
The same crooked smile.

I feel myself
smile back.

But then my smile
wobbles
and falls away.

Dani isn't the only one
in the picture.
She's surrounded
by four other girls.

All of them
are posed
in a neat line.
All of them
are locking arms.

All of them
are flashing
bright smiles.

None of them
look anything
like me.

Ghosts

I snap
my laptop
closed.
I push away
from my desk.

I grab
my phone
off the nightstand
and flop onto
my bed.

Ghostboy's comment
is waiting for me.
> *Do you think it's easier*
> *to like a ghost?*
> *Than it is to like*
> *a real live person?*

I lower my phone
and stare
up at the ceiling.

Ghostboy's question feels like
the edge of something.
Like the highest point
of a roller coaster.
Like a diving board.

I think about
Elena.

I think about
Dani.

I pick up
my phone.

I do,
I type.
I think it's easier
to like a ghost.

Because ghosts aren't
real.

Ghosts can't
let you down.

Ghosts can be
whatever
you want them
to be.

Another Message

My room
is dark
when I wake up.
Except for the
moonglow
of my phone screen.

I lie in bed
and stare at
the stack
of books
in the corner.
All my
unread books
look the same
in the faint light.
A row of
gray stripes
like ghostly fingers.

The word
ghost
echoes in my head.

I sit up.
I grab
my phone.

I look down
at my screen,
and my heart
jolts.

I have another message
from Ghostboy.

And this one
is
longer.

Ghostboy's Message

*You're right.
If ghosts are
made-up,
they can be
anything!*

*They are
a lot
like sand.
You can
shape them.*

*You can make
whatever
you like.*

Anyway . . .

*Which book
are you planning
to review
next?*

My Best

I sit in the car,
in the driveway.

I'm ready for school.
But Elena isn't.
She's still
inside the house.
She's making us late
again.

Mom leans over
and studies herself
in the rearview mirror.
I watch her
turn her face
this way
and that.

You look nice,
I say.

Mom smiles.
Thanks, she sighs.
I have an open house today.

*I want to put my
best foot forward.*

I want to look my best.

Doesn't Matter

A car horn blares.
A light turns red.
Smoke curls
from an exhaust pipe.

But in my head,
Ghostboy's words
are as soft
as creased pages.
As steady
as raindrops.

I close my eyes.
And it suddenly
doesn't matter
if Elena takes forever
to get ready.
It doesn't matter
that we're running late
because of her.

It all
runs
through my fingers
like sand.

Thanks a Lot

The late bell rings
just as Elena and I
walk in the front door.

Great, I sigh.
Now we're late.
Thanks a lot!

Elena hikes
her overstuffed backpack
higher
on her shoulders.
Her clarinet case
bangs her knee
as she shoves past me.
She reaches for
the main office
door.

She mutters
something.
I don't catch
what she says.
But it sounds
suspiciously like,
You're welcome.

Kites

A phone rings.
A keyboard clacks.
A copy machine whirs.
The main office
is like the center cog
in a giant engine.

Elena and I
take our place
at the counter.

I tell myself
I'm going to
stare
straight ahead.
I'm not
going to look.

But my eyes
are like kites,
tugged and pulled
by an invisible breeze.

My gaze drifts
to the back of the room.
Until it lands
at the far table.

Where Marco sits.

Must Be Nice

Marco runs his fingers
through the dark waves
of his hair.
He frowns down
at his phone.
He tips
his chair
back.

I hold my breath
like I'm watching
a tightrope act.
I wait for him
to lose
his balance.
To fall.

But he
never does.

Something sharp
bumps
my hip.
Elena's clarinet case.

Must be nice,
she mutters.

*To sit at a table
and play
with your phone
all morning.*

An unexpected laugh
spills out of my mouth.

Elena blinks at me.
Her face lights up
in one of her grins.

And then it's our turn
to pick up our
late slips.

Dear Ghostboy

*I haven't decided
which book I'll review
next.*

Maybe a poetry book?

Poetry

I look down
at what I've
just written.

I love reading
all types of books.
Especially
poetry books.

But poetry
won't get me
views.

Poetry
won't get me any
subscribers.

So I go back.
I delete
what I wrote.

Instead, I write:

> *I haven't decided
> which book I'll review
> next.*

Any suggestions?

Suggestions

Ghostboy's reply
arrives
one
hour
later.

> *I have*
> *so many*
> *suggestions!!*

Email Address

The reply is signed:
Ghostboy.
As usual.

But this time,
it's followed by
an email address.

My heart
skips
like a grocery cart
with a broken wheel.

The email address
is from
my school.

Ghostboy
is a student
at my school!

A Poet

I know I have to be
careful.
Ghostboy
is a stranger.

A
ghost
boy.

But I think
he's also
a poet.

He's good
with words.

And words are
the firefly sparks
that get me through
each
lonely
day.

For the First Time

I sit in the library
at lunch.
I huddle between rows
of dusty books.

I tap away
at my phone screen.
I type out an email
addressed to
Ghostboy.

I tell him about
my favorite books.
I ask about his.

For the first time
in a very
long
time,
I don't notice
if it's loud
or quiet.

For the first time,
I'm not
counting the minutes
until lunch is over.

For the first time
since Dani moved away,
I don't feel
lonely.

How Was Your Day?

Mom picks us up
after school.

How was your day?
she asks.

Great!
Elena squeals.

She chatters away
about band practice.
About her upcoming
halftime show
on the football field.
About football players.

I pull out my phone
and check my email.
I have an answer
from Ghostboy!

My heart cartwheels
in my chest.
I put my phone down.
I look out the window
and smile.

Maybe

*We're reading
a new book,*
Elena announces.
In English class.

There's a long stretch
of silence.
Then I realize
she's talking
to me.

I turn around.
Elena sits
in the back seat.
Her giant backpack
on her lap.

*Maybe I could see
your notes*, she says.
*From when you took
the same class
last year.*

Not a chance,
I start to say.
But then I change
my mind.

It's been a long time
since Elena
needed me.

It's been a long time
since she asked
for my help.

Sure,
I say instead.
Maybe.

Mom tucks a strand
of glossy black hair
behind her ear.

That's nice, Gabby,
she says.
*I like when you girls
get along.*

Elena rolls her eyes
at me.
I make a face
at her.
I turn back
to face the front.
But not before I hear
the soft happy
huff
of Elena's laughter.

Suggestions

Ghostboy's email
is short.

*What are you
up to
this weekend?*
he asks.

Then he drops a list
of his top three books.
These are my suggestions,
he writes.
For your next review.

I skim the book titles.
    A biography.
    A high fantasy.
    A collection of essays.

I've read them
all.

And I loved
every
one
of
them.

Even

Saturday morning,
Mom knocks
on my door.
*I need you to go
dress shopping
with your sister.*

I frown at her.
Why me?

*I have to
show a house,*
she says.
*And your father
has meetings
all day.*

*What about
Elena's friends?*
I whine.

My friends are busy,
Elena calls
from somewhere
down the hall.

I look at Mom.
Fine, I sigh.
But you owe me.

My mom winks
one perfectly lined eye.
I gave you life,
she says.
I think we're even.

Emails

Dear Ghostboy,

*My plans
this weekend
are to go dress shopping
with my little sister.*

*It's my own
personal version
of torture.*

*Is there anything worse
than little sisters?*

    Dear Gabby,

    *Yes.
    There's something worse.
    An older brother
    in medical school.*

    *My parents
    love to ask
    if I'm going to be
    a surgeon.
    Just like my
    perfect
    older brother.*

Spoiler: I'm not.

*I'm going to be
a famous
photographer. ;)*

What about you?

Ghostboy,

That's awesome!

I think photographers
are just as important
as doctors.

I'm going to be
a writer.
A poet.

Like Pablo Neruda.
Like Elizabeth Acevedo.

Gabby!!!

*Those are
two of my favorite
poets!*

*I'd love to see
your poetry
someday.*

*So . . .
Dress shopping
with your sister . . .*

*Are you buying
a dress too?*

Ghost,

Nope.

No dress for me.

*I'm not going
to homecoming.*

Gabs,

*Why aren't you going
to homecoming?*

An Apron

Mom drops us off
at the mall.

*Remember last time
we did this?*
Elena asks.

I bite my lip
to catch a smile.
I was 13.
And Elena
had been about to turn
12.

You refused to leave,
I snort,
*until I bought you
that apron
from the kitchen store.*

It had kittens on it!
Elena cries.

I laugh,
remembering Mom's face.
She had expected us to buy
a dress
for Elena's birthday party.

Instead,
we came home
with a five-dollar apron.

*Maybe we can find you
another apron,*
I say.
A nicer one.
For homecoming.

Elena bumps
my shoulder.
I bump hers.

I think about asking her
about Justin.
> How did she meet him?
> How are they friends?
> Why didn't she
> tell me?

But then
I change my mind.

Because
for a minute,
things are almost like
they used to be
when Elena
was turning
12.

When I bought her
an apron
with kittens on it.
When that made me
her hero.

Fitting Room

I sit
on a narrow couch
outside the fitting room.

Hurry up!
I call out.

I'm hurrying!
Elena snaps
from one of the
changing rooms.

I swallow a sigh
and pull out my phone.
I open my email.

Ghostboy's question
sits in my inbox.
Patiently waiting.
*Why aren't you going
to homecoming?*

The Reason

I give Ghostboy
a list of reasons
I'm not going
to homecoming.
> *I don't like dress shopping.*
> *I don't like crowds.*
> *I don't like loud music.*

Then I give him
the biggest reason.
> *I don't have anyone*
> *to go with.*

> *Maybe things would be*
> *different,*
> I write,
> *if I still had*
> *a best friend.*

> *But my best friend*
> *moved away.*

> *So now,*
> *I don't have*
> *anyone.*

Dear Gabby,

*I know what it's like
to lose a friend.*

*But I'm sure
you have
someone.*

*At the very least,
you have
me. :)*

*Your friend,
Ghostboy*

Cupcake

I look up
and see Elena
standing in front of me.

She's wearing
a pink dress.
       Puffy sleeves.
       A-line skirt.
       Lots of tulle.

Wow,
I snort.
*You look like
a melted cupcake.*

I wait for Elena
to laugh.
Or scowl.
Or roll her eyes.

Instead,
she points
at my phone.
She tips her head
to one side.
She asks,
Who's Ghostboy?

Someone

I scramble
to tuck my phone
back in my purse.

Someone
from school,
I sputter.

Someone
I know.

Just
someone
who's
a friend.

Over and Over

That night,
I lie in bed.
I hold my phone
in both hands
like it might slip
through my fingers.

I read
Ghostboy's email
over and over.

I know what it's like . . .

> *. . . you have someone.*

> *. . . you have me.*

Just So You Know

On the way to school,
Mom turns up
the radio.
I brace myself
for Elena's singing.
Instead,
Elena grabs
the back of my seat.
She leans forward.
She taps my arm.

That's a fake account,
she hisses.
Just so you know.

I turn around.
*What are you
talking about?*

Ghostboy,
she whispers.
He's not real.

I narrow my eyes.
*I told you!
He's someone
from school.*

Obviously!
Elena sniffs.
But all student emails
start with a first initial.
Then a last name.

That one
doesn't.

That one just says
Ghostboy.

Elena's Words

Elena's words
follow me
all the way
to homeroom.

They sit
in my head
while I'm taking
my science quiz.
They whisper
in my ear.
They float
at the edge
of the paper.

When first period ends,
I pull out my phone.

I type out a quick email.
> *Are you*
> *in school*
> *today?*

Ghostboy's reply
arrives five minutes
later.

I'm here, it says.
*Do you want
to eat lunch
together?*

Spinning Stories

I tell Ghostboy
I eat lunch
in the library.

And then I spend
the rest
of second period
spinning stories
in my head.

I picture us
eating lunch
together.
I imagine us
sitting
between the rows
of books.
I think about
the silence
that always hangs
over the library.
And how we'll break it
with our whispers.
  Our stories.
    Our laughter.

Less Than Two Hours

I glide
into third period
like a bird
skimming
across the sky.
I slide
into my chair
and look at the clock.

In less than
two hours,
I'll be eating lunch
with Ghostboy.

I press my lips together
to trap a smile.
I hardly notice
the steady hum
of conversation
around me.
It barely bothers me
that none
of the conversations
include me.

I Won't Be Disappointed

I do my best
not to paint
a mental picture
of Ghostboy.
That way,
I won't be disappointed
if his smile
isn't easy
and warm.
Or if his eyes
aren't kind.

I don't think about
what Ghostboy
is expecting,
either.
Not until an hour
before lunchtime.
And then it hits me
like a brick.

What is Ghostboy
hoping for?

Best Foot Forward

My stomach
flutters
with worry.

I don't know
who Ghostboy is.
I don't know
what he likes.
Or what he doesn't like.

Doubt creeps in.
But then I remember Dad
sliding on his suit jacket
each morning.
Carefully smoothing
his tie.

I remember Mom
fixing her makeup
in the rearview mirror.
So she can put
her best foot
forward.

I realize
I could do
the same.

I could find out
who Ghostboy is.
I can find out
his interests.

That way
I'll know
what to talk about.

I can be
the best version
of me.

I can put
my best foot
forward.

My Turn

The office
is quiet
during class time.
There are no students
waiting at the counter.
The table where
the student aides sit
is empty.

The secretary
is busy
on a call.
So I take a deep breath
and wait my turn.

I tap my hall pass
nervously
on the counter.
I glance at the clock.
I wonder if,
maybe,
this was a bad idea.

The secretary
waves her hand.
She snaps her fingers
at someone
behind me.

*Can you find out
what this young lady
needs?*

I turn around.
Only to find
Marco Acosta
standing
right
behind
me.

And I melt
into a puddle
on the floor.

I Need Help

I don't really
melt.
But when Marco says,
What's up?
I kind of wish
I could.

I lean
casually
against the counter.
Hi, I say.
I need help.

Marco quirks
one dark eyebrow.
What kind of help?

I tell myself
to be cool.
I tell myself
to stop staring
at his eyebrows.
*I need to find out
who an email address
belongs to,*
I say.

Marco nods.
What's the email address?

I gather
my courage.
Ghostboy, I blurt.
*That's the name
on the email address.*

Marco blinks at me.
Why do you want to know?

He's a friend,
I say.
*At least,
I think he is.*

Marco's lips
curl in a slow smile.
Okay, he says.

I let out a breath.
You'll look it up?

He shakes his head.
I don't have to.

*I created
that email address.*

I'm Ghostboy.

Oh...

It feels like
years pass
before I remember how
to speak.

Are you kidding?
I finally ask.

Marco shakes his head.
I'm not kidding, Gabby.
It's really me.

Oh, I say.
And then I say,
Oh...

Words are
the firework pops
that guide me
through dark days.

But on this day
they seem to have
abandoned me.

No Problem

The bell rings.

I bite back
a yelp
of surprise.

I have to go,
I stammer.

Marco grins.
No problem,
he says.
*I'll see you
at lunch.*

Ghostboy Is Marco

I spend the hour
before lunch
feeling like
a Ping-pong ball.

On the one hand,
Ghostboy is Marco.

MARCO!

I've had a crush on Marco
for as long as he's existed.
(Or at least,
for as long as
I've known
he exists.)

But
on the other hand,
Ghostboy
      is
            Marco.

Marco,
who runs the most popular
video channel
in school.

Marco,
who shares
everyone's secrets.

Marco,
who has never
once
spoken to me.

Freeze

At lunchtime,
I throw my backpack on.
I rake my fingers
through my bangs.
Then I march
to the library
to meet Marco.

But when I get
to the door,
I freeze.

My stomach
is one giant knot.
My heart
is a whole drum set.
I have the same
sick,
clammy feeling
I get
at the dentist.

I close my eyes.
I try to think about
Ghostboy's emails.
Ghostboy's words.

But all I can see
is Marco.

All I can think about
is how he created
a fake email account.
How I didn't realize
who I was
writing to.

How the person I thought
I was writing to
doesn't even exist.

In the End

I take a deep breath
and try
to just
walk
into the library.

But
in the end,
I can't.

In the end,
I eat lunch
in the auditorium.

I tuck myself
into one of the
folding seats.

I slide down
until I'm almost
invisible.

In the end,
I eat lunch
alone.

What Happened?

Dear Gabby,

*I thought
we were having lunch
together
today.*

*Is everything
okay?*

What happened?

- Ghostboy (aka Marco)

On and On

On the car ride home,
I stare
out the window.
I study the clouds
gathering in the sky.
I do my best
to tune Elena
out.

But Elena
is going
on and on
about
homecoming.
About how it's only
four days
away.
About Justin . . .

Every time
she says
Justin's name,
I think about Marco.
I think about
the last video
he posted.
I think about him
saying Elena's name.

Spit Happens

I twist in my seat
to look at Elena.

She doesn't notice.
She just goes right on
chattering.

My eyes catch
on her clarinet case.
It's covered
in stickers.
A flower.
> A peace sign.
> A picture of a clarinet
> under the words
> SPIT HAPPENS.

I snort.
I shake my head.

What?
she says.

I realize
she's stopped talking.
She's frowning
at me.

I look at her sticker.
I look at her giant backpack.
I look at her.

*Why did Justin ask
you
to homecoming?*

Mom gasps,
Gabby!

Silence
fills the car.

I look at Elena's
crumpled face.
And I realize
what I just said.
I realize how mean
it sounded.

I try to explain.
*It's just that
Justin is so cool—*

Gabriela!
Mom snaps
before I can say
anything more.
*Gabriela,
that's enough.*

The Last Meatball

During dinner,
Dad tells us
about the building
he's designing
for a new client.

Mom talks about
all the new houses
going up for sale.

The two of them
fill the silence
between
clinking forks.
But
it still feels
strangely
quiet.

I look over
at Elena.

She's staring down
at her plate.
She's pushing her
spaghetti
around and around.

I realize
she hasn't tried
to steal
the last meatball.
She hasn't mentioned
homecoming.
She hasn't teased me
about my vlog.

She hasn't
said
anything.

Blank

That night,
I sit in front of
my laptop.

I think about
recording
a new vlog post.
But each time
I look
at my bookshelves,
I remember Ghostboy's
book suggestions.

I open up
my email.
~~Ghostboy's~~ Marco's
message
is still sitting
in my inbox:
      What happened?

My fingertips
find my keyboard.

But when I try
to answer his question,
my mind goes
completely
blank.

Writing to Marco

Writing to Ghostboy
was easy.

Ghostboy
was good with words.

We liked
the same books.

When he talked
about ghosts,
he sounded sad.
He sounded a little lonely.
He sounded
like me.

But writing to Marco
is different.

Marco is
the most popular guy
in school.

He isn't
sad.

And he
certainly
isn't lonely.

Nothing New

I lose myself
in social media
for a little while.

I disappear
into pictures
of bookshelves.
       A sleeping cat.
            Someone's matcha latte.

After a while,
I realize
I haven't seen
a new post
from Dani.

I scroll
for several minutes.
I check her account.
But there's
nothing new.
There's nothing
after the last picture.
The one with
her new friends.
The one where
she was
smiling.

An Alert

On the way to school,
my phone
chimes
an alert.

I check
the notification
on my screen.
And my stomach
flounders
and
dips.

Marco
        just uploaded
                a new video.

Wait

I mumble
a quick goodbye
as I slam the car door.

Gabby,
Mom calls.
Wait for your sister!

But I pretend
I don't hear her.

I fast-walk
into the school.
I hurry past
the main office.
I make my way
to the library.
And then I slip inside.

A Scratchy Old Sweater

The silence in the library
folds over me
like a scratchy old sweater
as soon as the door
falls closed.

I only have
eight minutes
until the bell rings.
But I weave
between rows of books
until I find
my usual spot.

I drop my backpack
and sink
to the ground.
I hug my knees
to my chest.
And I watch
Marco's video.

He Tells the World

Marco's latest video
is all about
homecoming.
        Who asked who?
        Who accepted?

Marco's voice
reveals all the details.
But all the screen shows
is a photograph
of a broken-down car.
        An empty bus.
               A single flower
               poking through
               a crack in the pavement.

When I hear
Elena's name,
my breath catches
in my throat.

Marco reminds everyone
that Elena is going
to homecoming
with Justin.

Then he takes
a deep breath.

And he tells
the world
that Elena went
dress shopping.

He tells
everyone
about her pink dress.
How much
I hated it.
How I said she looked
just like
a melted cupcake.

One of My Secrets

The silence
after the video ends
feels like a scarf
pulled way
too
tight.

Marco
just went online
and told everyone
something I shared
with Ghostboy.

Marco just took
one of my secrets
and held it up
for all the world
to see.

Everything I Wrote

My heart feels like
one of Elena's
metronomes.

Tick tick tick . . .

I open up my email
and scroll back
through my messages.

I look at
everything
Marco wrote.
      I look at
      everything
      I wrote back.

My stomach
becomes a ship
sinking
right
down
to the ocean floor.

The girl in my emails
doesn't have
any friends.

She's not sparkly
or bubbly.
She's not fun.

The Gabby
in my emails
isn't the Gabby
I want the world
to see.

But there's
nothing
to stop Marco
from showing her
to everyone
anyway.

Information

I don't answer
Marco's email.

Even after
morning announcements,
when I hear people
whispering
about his latest video.

Even after
second period,
when I overhear
my sister's name.

I whip out
my phone.
I type
a quick message.
> *Dear Marco,*
> *I don't want*
> *what I write*
> *to end up*
> *in your videos.*

But I don't
send it.

Because
even that
feels like
information
he could use.

Even that
feels like
a secret.

All I Remember

That night
I force myself
to choose a book
off my shelf.
>A bestseller
>about a bank heist.
>A thriller
>with a lot of action.
>A lot of plot twists.

I sit down
in front of my laptop.
I try to record
a review.

But I don't remember
much
about the book.

All I remember
is that I had to
force myself
to read it.

All I remember
is that it didn't have
any
poetry.

Waiting for Elena

Mom drops us off
in front of the school
with a wave.

I stand on the sidewalk
and wait
for Elena.

But Elena
fiddles with
her backpack straps.
She fumbles with
her clarinet case.
She makes a big show
of pushing the car door
closed.

After a while,
I spin away.
I start to walk in
without her.

But I only manage
two steps
before I'm forced to stop.

Hey

Marco stands
in front of me
on the sidewalk.

Hey,
he says.

So I say,
Hey.

He nods a greeting
at someone
over my shoulder.
I turn
in time to see Elena
nod back.
And something
slides
into place
in my heart.

I turn back
to Marco.

*Why did you create
a fake email account?*
I demand.

Marco frowns.
His gaze
flicks
to Elena.
And my heart
plummets
like a star
falling out
of the sky.

That tiny flick
is all the answer
I needed.

I Figured It Out

Marco asks
if we can talk.

But I shake my head.
What for?
Do you need
more
information
about Elena?

Marco frowns.
What?

I roll my eyes.
It's okay,
I tell him.
I figured it out.

Elena is going
to homecoming
with your best friend.

And I
am Elena's
sister.

Marco's eyes
go wide.

*You think I created
a fake email account
so I could spy on you?*

I shrug.
*I never would have written
half of what I wrote
to Ghostboy.*

*Not if I knew
who I was really
writing to.*

Marco's face
goes as blank
as a carved statue.
        A piece of marble.
              An empty canvas.

I know,
he mutters.
He shoves his hands
in his pockets.
*It's easier
to like a ghost.*

He looks over my shoulder.
He nods at Elena.

And then he turns
and walks away.

I Remind Myself

My heart
curls
into a fist
as I watch Marco
disappear
into the crowd.
But I tell myself
not to cry.

>   I remind myself
>   of the way he talked
>   about Elena
>   on his vlog.

I remind myself
that he shared
my secrets.

I remind myself
that the only reason
he ever wrote to me
in the first place
was because
he wanted to know
about Elena.

There's a tiny part of me
that tries
to fight back.

Maybe,
it whispers,
*Marco wrote to you
because he liked
your book reviews.*

But I take a deep breath
and shove that voice
back
out
of my head.

I picture Marco
the way I usually
see him.
> Sitting at a table
> in the main office.
> Studying his phone.

I remind myself
what it felt like
to stand at the office counter,
wishing
he would look at me.

I remind myself
how he never
once
lifted his head.

All I Can See

I walk into
first period
like I'm wading
into an ocean.

My feet feel
heavy.
My steps are
slow.
My heart feels
like a torn
piece of paper.

I find my way to my desk
and fall into my chair.

I pull out
my notebook
and turn to a blank page.

But all I can see
is Marco's face.
The way his gaze
flicked
to Elena.
The way his forehead
furrowed.
How he walked
away.

Seaweed

Bits of conversation
find their way to me.
Like seaweed
washing up
on a shore.
      Homecoming . . .
            . . . Marco's video . . .
    . . . dress shopping.

I tell myself
they're talking about
Elena.
They're not talking about
me.

But that doesn't
make me feel
any better.

Words bounce
like ocean waves
against me.
I hold onto my pen
like I'm holding onto the edge
of a boat.
Like I'm trying to keep it
steady.
Like I'm trying
not to fall off.

Back Down

Right before class starts,
I pull out my phone.
I swipe through
my accounts.
        Email.
        Social media.
        Discord.

I open up my vlog
and glance
at my latest video.
        My review of
        the bank heist book.

My shoulders sag
when I realize
my video
doesn't have
a
single
view.

My eyes sweep
back up
to the top of the page.

I look at
my follower count.

And the world goes
completely
still.

Somebody
unfollowed
me.

My follower count
is back down
to two.

Subscribers

I study
the short list
of my subscribers.

I recognize
Mom's account
right away.
>   The one she created
>   just so
>   she could follow me.
>   *RealtorMom*.

I recognize
the spam account.
>   The one that has been
>   following me
>   since I started
>   my channel.
>   *Reedingisfun*.

But I don't see
Marco's account.
>   I don't see
>   *Ghostboy*.

Marco
unfollowed
me.

The Same Silence

The library is quiet
at lunchtime.
It's the same silence
that always
folds around me.
The kind that falls
like heavy curtains.

I sink into my usual spot
and dig my lunch
out of my backpack.

My phone
pings
an alert.
And my heart
bounces
like a rubber ball.

But it's just
a reminder
about my upcoming
math test.

All the Small Sounds

The clock
on the wall
marks the minutes.
The air conditioning
hums.
The overhead lights
buzz.

All the small sounds
bump up
against the silence
of the library.
They magnify it.
They make the silence
louder.

I try to break the silence
by tapping my fingers
on my knee.

But the minute I stop,
the silence
rushes
back in.
It surrounds me
like an ocean.
Like a giant wall.
Like the bars
of a cage.

The Bottom Shelf

When the bell rings,
I gather up
the remains
of my lunch.
I tuck my legs
under me
and get ready
to stand.

But right before
I do,
my eyes catch
on something.
A thin thread
of cobweb
on the bottom bookshelf.
A film of dust
on the books
sitting there.

I rock back
on my heels.

I know
just
how
those books feel.

I know exactly
what it's like
to sit
on the bottom shelf.
Day after day.

    Unnoticed.

        Forgotten.

            Unseen.

Time

After dinner,
I climb the stairs
to my room.
I think about working on
my vlog.
But in the end,
I don't.

I've spent so much time
trying to grow
my video channel.
I've put so much effort in
trying to get people
to watch.
But nothing
has changed.
No one
has noticed.

How It Is

Mom is sitting
at the kitchen counter.
But she looks up
when she hears me
on the stairs.

I sit next to her
at the counter.
I look down
and see she's reading
a postcard.

*Is that from
Dani's mom?*
I ask.

Mom nods.
But she doesn't smile.

I think about
my mom
and Dani's mom.
How close they were.
How they were a lot
like me and Dani.

Do you miss her?
I ask.

Mom sighs,
All the time.

*I hardly ever
hear from her.
And when I do,
it's just a postcard.*

But that's okay,
she says.
I know how it is.

I frown.
How is it?

Mom shrugs.
*Dani's mom has never learned
how to let people in.
Especially when
she's hurting.*

She looks at me
and a slow smile
softens her face.

*I think you know
what I mean,*
she says.
*I think Dani might be
a little like that,
too.*

Beautiful

Mom leans over
and brushes my bangs
out of my face.

*You should think about
pinning these
back,*
she says.

I pull away.
What for?

She shrugs.
*You're a beautiful girl.
You have my genes.*

I roll my eyes.
*That must be why
I'm so modest, too.*

Mom throws her head
back
and laughs
one of her
big
laughs.

The kind that
makes her eyes
crinkle
at the edges.

I look at my mom.
It occurs to me
that only the people
closest
to her
get to see her this way.

No makeup.
Jogging pants.
A huge grin
plastered
on her beautiful face.

Someone Knocks

Right before bedtime,
someone knocks
on my door.

I look up,
expecting Mom.
Or Dad.

Instead,
Elena pokes her head
inside.

I'm the One

Elena scans
my bookshelves.
My nightstand.
Her gaze drifts
down
to the pile
of unread books
in the corner.

She takes
a deep breath
and puffs out
her cheeks.

In that moment,
she looks
just like she did
when she was
eight.
When she used to
run to my room
during a thunderstorm.

I feel my lips
twitch
in a smile.

But then Elena says,
I'm the one
who told Marco
about your book reviews.

I'm the one
who showed him
your videos.

And the smile
slides
right
off
my face.

All I Had to Do

Elena tries
to escape
to her room.
But I slip inside
before she can
close the door.

I cry,
*What the heck,
Elena?*

My sister
spins around.
*I'm sorry!
I knew
how much
you liked him.*

My mouth falls open.
How?

Elena shrugs.
*I saw your face
whenever he was around.*

*So you told him
I like him?*
I huff.

Elena scowls.
No way!
I just told him
about your vlog.

I fold my arms
across my chest.
I don't get it.

Elena squints.
Which part?

All of it!
I shout.

Any
of
it . . .

How do you
know Marco?
How do you
know Justin?
How do
    you
        know
            anyone?

Kind of a Big Deal

Elena stares at me
for a really
long
time.

Gabby,
she says at last.
Justin is band captain.

I shrug.
So?

Elena shakes
her head.
So,
I just started
high school.
And I'm already
section leader.
      I'm already
      performing
      at halftime.
            I'm already
            first chair.

*Don't you think that's
kind of
a big deal?
Don't you think
I'm someone
worth knowing?*

What I See

I don't
really know
what to say
to Elena.
So I say
nothing.

I turn to go.
But on my way
out the door,
I pause.

Elena's dresser
is littered
with makeup.
        Sheet music
        is strewn across
        the floor.

Elena's room
is a disaster!

But that's not
what I see.

What I see is
everything
that's missing.

Her stuffed animals.
Her favorite doll.

What I see is
how much her room
changed
when I wasn't
looking.

What I Don't See

That night
I lie in bed,
staring up
at the ceiling.

I turn Mom's words
over and over
in my head.
The ones she said
about Dani's mom.
The ones she said
about Dani.

I try to imagine
what it feels like
to be Dani.
To be the new person
in a new school,
in a new country.

I sit up
and grab my phone.
I scroll through
the handful of pictures
Dani has posted
since she left.

I see coffee art.
A busy London street.
I see Dani
smiling.

But what I don't see
is what happens
when Dani isn't
in front of
the camera.
I can't see
the first day of school.
Or the first night
in her new house.

I realize
I'll never know
what Dani is going through.
Not if she won't
tell me.

I can't see
someone
who doesn't want to be
seen.

Love Always

I open up
my email
and type a quick message.

Dear Dani,
I miss you like crazy.
Love always,
(Seriously, ALWAYS!)
Gabby

I send my message.
And then I lie back
and close my eyes.
I know Dani
won't answer.
Not until
she's ready.
But at least she knows
I'm here
until then.

Books

Mom drops us off
at school
with her usual wave.

I hop out
and wait
while Elena
wrestles
with her giant backpack.

*What do you
even
have in there?*
I ask.

Elena shrugs.
Books.

I gasp.
*You have
that many
schoolbooks?*

Elena looks
down
at her feet.
They're library books.

Library books?
I say.
What for?

Elena's cheeks
turn the same shade of pink
as the cupcake dress
she tried on
at the mall.

*I try to read
all the books you review
on your channel,*
she mutters.
*But I don't read
as fast
as you do.*

*It's hard
for me
to keep up.*

See Me

I stand there
frowning at Elena
while Mom drives
away.

Wait a minute,
I finally say.
You don't even follow
my vlog.

Elena's mouth
falls open.

Sometimes,
she says,
I think
I could be standing
right between
you
and a stack of books.

And you still
wouldn't
see me
at all.

Reeding Is Fun

The bell rings.
We're officially
late for class.
But I can't seem
to make myself
move.

I look down
and see
Elena's clarinet case.

Clarinets.
Reeds.

My spam account.
Reedingisfun.

Reeding
is
fun.

Reedingisfun is Elena.

Noticed

I shake my head.
I didn't realize . . .

I know, Elena says.
You never do.

I open my mouth
to argue.
But then
I think about
Elena's room.
I think about
how long it took me
to realize
how much it's changed.

I've been so wrapped up
in my own loneliness
after Dani left.
I didn't even notice
my own sister.

But she
noticed
me.

Let Me Help

Elena does
a little hop.
Her giant backpack
bounces
on her shoulders.

Let me help you,
I say.

I don't need help,
Elena says.

I look at her
wrinkled nose.
Her squinty eyes.
She's not a little kid
anymore.
But she's still
my little sister.

I know you've got it,
I say.
But let me help
anyway.

Elena rolls her eyes.
Fine, she says.
Help away.

She hands me
her giant backpack.
And then she grins.

After You

We head to
the main office
together.
So we can pick up
our late slips.

When we get there,
Elena opens the door.

After you,
she says.

So I walk
through the door.
        Into the office.
                Right into Marco.

The Two of Us

Hey, Marco says.

Hey, I manage
to reply.

Hey! Elena pipes in.

She reaches out her hand.

My backpack,
she reminds me.

Oh, I say.
Right.

I hand it over and she winks at me.
Just like Mom always does.

Then she slides past me
toward the office counter.

She leaves
me and Marco
standing there
like statues.

She leaves the two of us
alone.

My Secrets

Marco's brown eyes
meet mine.
And I think of
gingerbread.
        Warm sand.
                Autumn leaves.

*Are you going to
accuse me
of spying
again?*
he asks.

I blink.
*That depends.
Are you going to share
any more
of my secrets?*

Marco scoffs.
What secrets?

Elena's dress?
I remind him.

Marco tips his head
to one side.
Elena told me that.

No, I argue.
I
told you that.

Marco frowns.
You told me
about dress shopping.

But Elena told me
about her dress.
She told me
what it looked like.
She told me
what you said.

I run
a gossip vlog,
Marco says.

But I don't share
people's secrets.

I don't share
anything
without permission.

Rest of the Day

The secretary
calls my name.

I look up
and see her holding
a piece of paper.
Your late slip,
she says.

I'll catch you later,
Marco tells me.

I nod.
Then I spend
the whole
rest of the day
hoping to see him.

But I don't even
catch
a glimpse.

Sonnets

That night,
I study
my bookshelves.

I have to post
another
book review.
>   Idle video channels
>   don't gain
>   followers.

But the book
I was going to
review
is awful.
>   A viral bestseller
>   about a magician.
>   Rambling.
>   Boring.
>   Dry.

I wander over
to the stack
of unread books
in the corner.
I grab the book
at the top
of the pile.

A book of sonnets.
A book of poetry.

I bought it because
I
love
poetry.
But I set it aside
because it didn't work
for my channel.
It wouldn't get me
any views.

But when I don't have
any views,
I don't have anything
to lose . . .

So I lift the cover
and flip
through the first few pages.

Words jump out at me.
Begging to be read.
So I flop
onto my bed
and read the first poem.
And then the next one.
And then the next.

A Perfect Version

I sit in my desk chair,
my laptop open
before me.
I look at the screen
and think about
all the hours I've spent
making videos.
All the time I've put in
trying to get noticed
by reviewing bestsellers
I didn't enjoy.

I close my eyes
and think of Dani
smiling
in every one
of her pictures.
I think of her
trying to be
a perfect version
of herself.
I think of the distance
it created
between us.
A distance
wider
than any ocean.

Welcome to My Channel

I pick up
my book of sonnets.

What if I forgot about
followers,
      views,
           likes?

What if I stopped
trying to be
some internet-famous version
of me?

What if I was
just
me?

I take a deep breath
and hit "record."

Welcome to my channel,
I say.

And then I
open up
my book of poems.

I Still Have Thoughts

After I upload
my new video,
I sit back
and close my eyes.

My heart is beating
like I just
stepped off a bus
onto an unfamiliar street.

But I also feel
something else.
Excited.
Relieved.
I have the same
soft, unwound feeling
I always get
when I throw off my jacket
after a snowy day.

I start to flip my laptop
closed.

But right before
it snaps shut,
I pause.

I still have
thoughts
fluttering around
my head.

I still have
things
I need
to say.

Ocean Waves

I take a minute
to catch my breath.

Then I look into
the camera
and hit "record."

Dear Marco,
I say.

Then
I fall
silent.

Words are
the match-strike flares
that get me through
each day.

But right now
they feel risky.
Uncertain.
Like ocean waves
that could tip
a boat
over.

Reflection

I lean in
and study my reflection
on the screen.

I think about
adding a filter.
I think about
editing the image.
I think about creating
a better version of myself.

But in the end,
I don't.

I don't want to shape myself
like sand.
I don't want to be
a ghost.

So I shake
my hands out.
I straighten
my shoulders.

I nod at the image of myself
on the screen.

And then I take a deep breath
and dive in.

Dear Marco . . .

I told you once
that it was easier
to like a ghost.

Because ghosts
can't let you down.

Ghosts
aren't real.

But I've learned
that you can't
love
a ghost.

You can't
love
someone
you can't
see.

A Secret

I stop recording.

My hands
are shaking.
My voice
is unsteady.

But I tell myself
to be brave.

I close my eyes.
I count to 10.

Then I open my eyes.
Hit "record."
And I tell Marco
a secret.

I tell him I've liked him
for as long as he's existed.
> (Or at least
> for as long as
> I've known
> he exists.)

*But the person I liked
was a ghost,
I admit.*

I never
talked to him.
He never
talked to me.

The person I liked
wasn't real.

I swallow
a nervous sigh.

But I'd like to
get to know you,
I tell him.

And I'd like for you
to know me,
too.

Who Marco Is

Marco Acosta
runs the most popular
gossip channel
in school.

But I'm not thinking
about that
when I email him
my video.
      When I email him
      my secret.

Marco told me
he doesn't share anything
without permission.
And I believe him.

Because, deep down,
I know who Marco is.

Marco is
a photographer.
A poet.

Marco is
Ghostboy.

And Ghostboy
is a friend.

Surprise!

The night of homecoming
I expect Elena
to flounce
down the stairs
in a cloud of pink.

Instead
she floats down
in a simple
black
gown.

*What happened
to the cupcake?*
I ask.

Elena grins
her braces-filled grin.
Surprise!

I smile
and shake my head.
*Why did you tell Marco
about the pink dress?*

Elena wags her eyebrows.
*You've got to keep
the people
on their toes!*

She does
a slow turn.
What do you think?

You look beautiful,
I tell her.

I do?
she asks.

I nod.
Of course you do!
Then, with a wink,
We share the same genes.

Big Reveal

The doorbell rings.
Elena waves me
toward it.

You get it,
she begs.
*Mom and Dad
have to record
my big reveal.*

I roll my eyes.
But I walk to the door
and pull it open.

Justin stands on the porch,
tugging at his sleeves.

Elena's sister?
he asks.

Yep, I sigh.
That's me.

Justin nods.
He gestures behind him.

*I think you know
my friend,
Marco.*

Homecoming

Justin's face lights up
when he spots Elena.
He drifts past me
into the house.
He leaves
me and Marco
alone
by the front door.

I look at Marco.
He's wearing jeans.
Sneakers.
A hoodie.
But he still looks
like a work of art.

His hair
reminds me
of a windswept field.

His eyes
make me think of
oak trees.

His eyebrows—

*What are you
doing here?*

Elena asks
from somewhere
behind me.

Marco blinks.
Oh . . .
I'm not going
to homecoming.

Elena huffs.
Why not?

Marco shrugs.
He looks at me
and his lips
curl
in a slow smile.

I don't like
loud music,
he says.
I don't like
crowds.

Looking

Mom insists
on taking pictures
of everyone.
Even Marco.

After what feels like
100 pictures,
she lowers her phone.
She dabs her eyes
and says,
Our girls are growing up.

Dad puts his arm
around her.
He offers up his sleeve.
Would you like a tissue?

Mom lets out
a messy
half-sob, half-laugh.

I dart
a nervous glance
at Marco.

But Marco
isn't looking
at my parents.

Marco
is looking
at me.

Of Course I Did

As we walk
to the front door,
Dad falls back
between me and Marco.

So, he says.
*What are you two
up to?*

I don't know,
Marco says.
*I brought my own car.
I thought
Gabby and I
could drive
to the bookstore.
I thought
we could buy
some more
poetry books.*

It takes me
a minute
to realize
what Marco just said.
    To realize
        what it means.

*You watched
my video!*
I cry.

Marco nods.
*Of course I did.
You run the best
book review channel
in the whole school.*

I take a deep breath.
*And you
run the best
photography vlog.*

Marco's eyes
go wide.
*You noticed
my pictures
in my videos?*

I look at him
and smile.
Of course I did.

The People Who See

On the way
out the door,
I hear Justin ask Elena
what kind of music
she wants to hear in the car.

I open my mouth
to warn Elena
not to sing
in front of Justin.

But then, I remember:
You can't love
what you can't see.

The people
who love you
are the people
who get to see
your messy side.
>	Your big laughs.
>	Your weird parents.
>	Your off-key singing.

So I snap my mouth
closed.

I stand next to Marco
and watch Elena
climb
into Justin's car.

I watch the car
pull out of the drive.

I watch
as it drives away.

I shield my eyes
against the setting sun.
And I keep watching
for as long as I can.

WANT TO KEEP READING?

If you liked this book, check out another book from West 44 Books:

DEFINITELY NOT A LOVE STORY BY CLAUDIA RECINOS SELDEEN

ISBN: 9781978597150

LOVE IS . . .

My mom writes
romance novels
in her stolen time.
Between doing dishes
and folding the laundry.

In her books,
love
conquers all.

But in real life,
love is just
a fairy tale
that pays the bills.

In real life,
love is
Mom and Dad.
Fighting.
A running whisper
of disagreement.
Like a hissing teakettle
that never boils.

Love is
my sister, Clara.
Locking herself
in her room
after another
breakup.

In Mom's stories,
love is
everything.

But in real life,
love is
a box
of tissues.

A closed
door.

Love is
something
I want no part of.

ANA BANANA

Regina calls,
Ana Banana!

So I shove my locker
closed.
I turn around.
The braid
of my hair
whipping
around my shoulders.

My name isn't really
Ana Banana.
It's Ana Morales.
No fruit involved.

But Regina
has been calling me
Ana Banana
since first grade.

It's like
our secret handshake.
A code.

It's the password
that lets her into
the VIP room
of my heart.

DID YOU FORGET?

Regina is grinning.
A wide grin.
As boundless
as the ocean.

What's up?
I ask.
*Did you and Olivia
make up?*

Regina and her girlfriend
are like a roller coaster.
Ups and downs.
Twists and turns.
Lots of screaming.

Regina blushes.
Making the dusting
of freckles
on her cheeks
stand out
like exclamation points.

No! she says.
*I mean, yes.
But that's not why
I'm smiling.*

*Then why
are you smiling?*
I ask.

Regina's face
dims.

Dress shopping!
she cries.
After school!
Did you forget?

I reach up
and tug playfully
on one of
her curls.

Don't worry,
I say.
I didn't forget.

CHECK OUT MORE BOOKS AT:
www.west44books.com

An imprint of Enslow Publishing

WEST **44** BOOKS™

About the Author

Claudia is the author of several young adult verse novels including *Definitely Not a Love Story* and *To Be Maya*. Her work has appeared in *The Amphibian Literary Journal* and *First Peoples Shared Stories*. Claudia is a first generation Guatemalan American. When not writing, she is either playing video games with her husband and son or chasing after the family cats. Find out more at: www.recinosseldeen.com.